The Song of the Ocean

The Song of the Ocean

Gianna Perugini

ISBN: 1537127810
ISBN 13: 9781537127811
Library of Congress Control Number: 2016913678
CreateSpace Independent Publishing Platform
North Charleston, South Carolina

Chapter 1

The alarm was going off. I looked at the clock. It read 6:00 a.m. "Uhhhh," I muttered and rolled out of bed. I'm so not a morning person. I looked up though and saw my light-blue suitcase sitting in the corner of the room. My usual grumpy morning spirit turned into a smile, and I grabbed my outfit, which I had laid out the night before. I quickly got ready, grabbed my luggage, and ran out the door of my room. I dragged my heavy suitcase down the stairs, screaming, "Mommm, I'm ready to go!"

"Sweetie, it's not time to go yet! We still have another hour," she replied.

I frowned and brought my suitcase to the front door.

"OK, I'll be in my room then," I said, sighing. I grabbed my cell phone and dialed the number of my best friend, Jenny, and she answered on the first ring.

"Ha-ha, I was just about to call you." She laughed. "I'm so excited. I honestly can't believe that we both got in to this camp." Jenny and I talked for a little while more before she had to go eat breakfast. I told her to text me when she was on her way. I hung up the phone and flopped back onto the bed. Jenny and I did a lot together, and most of it had to do with dolphins. Now, we had both been accepted into this elite camp for future marine biologists. There were thousands of applicants, but only four sixth graders were chosen. It was so awesome that I got picked, but having my best friend with me made it even better.

I decided to read the camp brochure one last time before leaving for the trip. I was reading the last page of the brochure when my mom walked in and said, "Lily, it's time to go."

I jumped out of bed, grabbed my cell phone, and ran past her, down the stairs, and to the living room, where my dad was lying on the couch. I hugged him good-bye and slipped on my shoes. I waited at the front door for my mom. "Mommm, are you coming?" My mom laughed.

I suddenly heard my little brother, Anthony. "I want to come! I want to come!" My mom smiled and agreed that he could. I opened the door, pulled my suitcase behind me, and walked to the car. My mom helped me load up my luggage, and I jumped into the car with my cell phone. I spotted my diary sitting on the passenger seat. "Oops! I would have forgotten this," I said, opening my diary and beginning to write.

Dear Diary,

Today is June 2, and yesterday was super busy! I spent it packing for camp. It took me six hours, although I did take breaks to eat breakfast, lunch, and dinner. The whole thing may sound crazy, but really it's just the start of the biggest summer of my life. I am on my way now, so I will write more later.

The drive from where I lived, in the Tampa Bay area, to Miami was five hours long, and honestly I thought we would never get there. I played every game on my phone and read some articles about whales.

"Do you guys want to watch a movie?" my mom asked.

"Sure!" I replied, hoping it would make the time pass quicker. I turned on the movie and put on my headphones. Anthony did the same. By the end of the movie, we were pulling into the marina. I looked out of the window and saw the boat. I was so excited I wanted to jump out of the car. My mom pulled to a stop, and I slipped my diary and cell phone into my suitcase. I then unloaded it and hugged my mom and brother good-bye.

"Bye! Love you! Be safe! Call me whenever you get cell service!" my mom said while my brother just said, "Bye, sissy!" I waved good-bye to them both and started walking over to the boat at the dock.

Chapter 2

I saw Jenny already standing on the dock, waiting. Next to her were two other girls, both dressed in name-brand clothes. One of the girls was smiling and talking really quickly to Jenny. The other one had a grumpy look on her face, and her arms were crossed. I stepped onto the dock and breathed in the salty smell of the ocean.

One of the girls said, "Aren't you guys so excited? Like I seriously can't wait. I hope we see lots of dolphins! Oh yes, lots of whales too." If I had to, I would have guessed that the girl talking to us was very sporty. She wore a pair of shorts and a T-shirt. Her hair was blond, cut to medium length, and tied in a messy ponytail. The one thing other than her appearance that I noticed was she never stopped talking.

"Um, can you slow down a second? What's your name?" I cut in between her words.

"Ah, my name. Thanks for reminding me. My name is Roxy! Roxy Fendricks. I'm a future marine biologist who absolutely loves dolphins. I like them more than whales, sharks, fish, and humans," Roxy replied. I looked over at Jenny, who raised her eyebrows.

"Does she ever shut up?" I whispered.

"I don't know, but I hope so, 'cause I can't listen to her much longer," Jenny replied. I looked at Roxy.

"Do you know who that is?" I said, pointing at the other girl, who was standing there, twirling her hair with a bored look on her face.

"Oh, that's my twin sister, Rose. She doesn't exactly like marine life, but my parents made her apply for the camp. They're both marine biologists, so they want us to follow in their footsteps."

Roxy chatted more. I looked her sister up and down. Her hair was curled to perfection; I couldn't find one frizz. She wore a nice flowered dress that stopped right above the knee, with a pair of flats to finish her outfit off.

"Hi! I'm Lily," I said to her. She looked at me, disgusted.

"Um, yeah, I'm Rose. Do you know when they are going to let us on this boat? I can't stand this heat. It's killing me."

I rolled my eyes and looked at my watch. "Five minutes, but it could be earlier, could be later." She rolled her eyes and went back to twirling her hair. What a diva, I thought to myself. I started to chit-chat with Jenny, when I heard a big splash.

"OMG…I'm wet now!" Rose exclaimed, looking down at her dress. I ran to the other side of the dock, near Rose, and saw the shape of a nurse shark gliding through the water next to the dock.

"It's a nurse shark!" I laughed.

"A…a shark? Get it away from me," she said, running off the dock onto the shore. Jenny and I laughed. Roxy just kept on talking.

"Nurse sharks are bottom-feeders and live off the coast of Florida. They usually stay on coastlines and beaches in the shallower waters."

I rolled my eyes, and Jenny said, "OK, we all know about nurse sharks, Roxy."

A middle-aged man walked along the boat deck with a boy about my age. "Hello, I'm Captain Frank, and this is my son Ash," he said. Ash waved at the mention of his name. "Ash won't be traveling with us, but he is here to help you girls bring all your stuff aboard. You may now board *Dolphin Dancer*," he said and let us board the ship.

We all stood on the deck of the ship, looking around. "OK, girls, I'm going to let you know your cabin number and roommate. I highly recommend you leave your fans running even when you're not in the room as there is no air conditioning. Roxy and Rose, you are in cabin one. Jenny and Lily, you are in cabin two." He paused. Jenny and I hugged. "Go down to your cabins and start to unpack. We will launch at four o'clock."

In the cabin, I looked at the cabin clock and saw we had a half hour of unpacking time till launch. By the time we were done, the room was totally dolphin themed, and Roxy was yelling to us that we were about to launch.

We walked up the stairs and onto the deck. The water was amazing, and the wind was perfect for sailing. The captain untied the rope, and we were off. It felt so good to be on the water with the breeze brushing past my face. We sat on the deck for a while just looking out into the open ocean. By now, *Dolphin Dancer* was pretty far out for having been sailing only an hour. Then I saw a pod of Atlantic bottlenose dolphins, their dark-gray fins cutting the surface of the water.

"Dolphins!" I yelled.

Jenny, Roxy, and Rose leaned on the railing to get a better look. The dolphins leaped and surfed on the waves before they disappeared underwater.

It was dinnertime now, so we headed toward the dining cabin. We were eating dinner when we heard voices. We went up on the deck and saw a boat approaching. I read the name on the side of the ship.

"Ahoy, *Wave Crasher*," we called.

"Ahoy," they called back.

They passed by us, but we were not happy to see what we saw—mounds of fish.

"Hey, I think you might have overfished," I yelled.

They had a net full of fish being reeled in by a machine when suddenly a large tiger shark came up with a large breach and grabbed the end of the net. The edge of boat was pulled underwater from the initial grab and then bobbed back up. Most of the fish fell out of the net and into the water.

Roxy said, "Wow!" as she watched in amazement as the shark swam away.

I looked at her and said, "Well, that might have been cool, but we have no video proof, so it's just a tale to be told." In my mind, though, I was thinking, yeah, that was so cool.

Jenny was jumping and saying, "I caught that on video."

We all looked at her and said, "What!"

"Caught it in 3-D, too!" she said cheerfully.

"Can we watch?" I said.

"Of course," she said, looking at me with a "why couldn't you?" expression.

Then Roxy said, "I thought that you thought it was just a tale to be told."

I shrugged and turned back to Jenny, and she said, "I'll send it to each of you."

It was getting late, so I wanted to head down to my cabin to get some rest. I walked into the room and got into the bottom bunk. I was lying there, resting, when I must have dozed off from the rocking of the ship.

The next thing I knew, Jenny was standing next to my bed, saying, "Get up, sleepyhead."

I couldn't believe it was already morning. I went ahead and got myself cleaned up, dressed, and ready to start my day. Just as I opened the cabin door to head to the dining area, Roxy caught sight of me. "Hey, Lily, wait! Wait for me!" She talked my ear off the entire walk, which probably was only five minutes, but listening to her made it seem like forever.

We went into the dining cabin and sat around the round wooden table. We ate breakfast and talked about all the exciting stuff we might learn about today.

My phone started ringing, and I grabbed it out of my pocket and answered it. "Hi," I said.

"Hey!" said the guy on the other end.

"Hi, Jeff," I said, giggling. Jeff and I were long-distance dating while I was on the trip.

"I know you just left for your trip, but I'm going to have to break up with you. My mom says that long-distance relationships don't usually work, and I really agree. I went to the mall and kinda was checking out other girls," he said. "So if you are only gone one day, and I am already doing this, I think it is for the best to end it."

"OK, well, it is your loss," I replied. I hung up the phone and started to cry. The girls were staring at me like, what happened? I said, "I can't believe he just did that. We should have just broken up before I left. What a jerk!" I ran down the stairs and into my cabin. I couldn't understand how he could have waited until one of the most exciting days of my life. Why couldn't he have done it before-hand? Before I was living my dream?

I looked at my wall and scanned it for the picture of Jeff and me. I ripped it off my wall and tore it up, throwing the scraps in the trash bin. I rubbed my eyes, and my throat was sore from trying to hold back the tears. It was one of those painful cries where you don't want to cry but can't hold it in. I lay down on my bed and let the tears flow out of me.

I don't know how long I was in the cabin, but Jenny and the others walked in, worried. When she saw my eyes were red, she asked, "What's wrong?"

I looked up at them and said, "Jeff broke up with me," in an unsteady voice.

The girls looked at me and said, "If he was any kind of guy, he wouldn't have broken up with you."

"It wasn't just him. It was also his mother," I said in a small voice.

Chapter 3

I wiped the corners of my eyes and said, "You know, his mother has wanted him to break up with me since the first day we met."

"His mother didn't like you?" asked Jenny, sitting down on the end of my bed.

The tears stung my eyes. "Yeah, when I first met her, we went out to eat, and she sat across from me. We were eating, and I had to go to the restroom. When I went to get up, I put my weight on the table, and it tipped over. Everything spilled on me, and I was so embarrassed. His mother got up and stormed out of the pizzeria."

Jenny looked surprised and said, "I'm surprised he didn't break up with you then."

I glared at her. "Not helping." I flopped back on the bed.

Jenny got up, and the girls slowly walked out of the room. I didn't want to waste my first day on the water crying over Jeff, so I sat up and took out my journal.

Dear Diary,
    Today is June 3, and Jeff broke up with me, and I don't know what to do about it. Long-distance relationships never work out anyway, right?

I got out of bed and walked to the underwater viewing center. The boat was really large, probably eighty feet long. It had four cabins, a glass room to view underwater, a dining room, a surgical room, and a giant deck pool in case we rescued any marine life while at camp. I was surprised to see Jenny was there, too.

"You missed the shark," Jenny said.

"What species?" I asked curiously.

"Black tip...I think."

I sat in one of the fluffy blue seats and watched as fish swam by. Large and small stingrays swam in the distance, nearly invisible, but I had a good eye when it came to spotting marine life. All of a sudden, I spotted something that made me stand up and take a picture with my camera. I watched as the sleek gray body of an Atlantic bottlenose dolphin swam by the glass room. Just like every other time I'd seen a dolphin, my heart lifted. The feeling had become so natural to me since I'd started wanting to become a marine biologist. I forgot about everything. I forgot there were other girls on the boat who would want to see the lonely dolphin. I forgot that Jeff had broken up with me. It was just me and that dolphin. The only thing separating us was the glass of the underwater viewing area. The dolphin looked at me curiously, and I looked right back. The dolphin's small black eyes had such intelligence behind them. The dolphin even swam over to the glass and pushed its rostrum (nose) against it. I snapped a photo. The dolphin was small, probably just a youngster. I knew something was wrong.

I was shaken out of my trance when I noticed a deep cut on the tail fluke and that the top part of the dorsal fin was sliced off. I ran upstairs as fast as I could, screaming orders at my friends. I grabbed my diving gear and a medic kit. My friends did the same—except for Jenny. She got the pool on deck ready for the (hopefully) temporary resident. This was not your standard pool. It was huge and took up the entire front end of the boat deck. It was for use only in an emergency, but this would be one. The captain stood by to make sure we did everything correctly, and in case we needed help.

I finished putting on my wet suit and flippers and dove in. I didn't need an oxygen tank, because I wouldn't really be underwater for that long. The young dolphin fought a bit, but eventually, we were able to gently glide it into the sling to get it out of the water and into the pool Jenny had set up. We then determined that the dolphin was female.

I got into the pool and carried the dolphin around so she wouldn't have to use as much strength to swim and wouldn't tire out. The young dolphin whistled lightly, occasionally letting out a small breath. We used umbrellas to create shade over the pool so the dolphin wouldn't get sunburned. I looked down at her slick gray head and whispered that she was going to be all right, even though I couldn't make any promises.

The young dolphin must have heard the uncertainty in my voice, because she started to get restless. She smacked her injured tail on the water repeatedly. I knew she had to stop.

I yelled for Jenny to come. She must have not heard me, because there was no response. I started to panic and began to stroke the top of the dolphin's head and sing, "Sweet little baby, don't you cry. Mama's going to sing you a lullaby." The dolphin slowly calmed down, and after I'd repeated the verse ten times, she lay still in my arms again.

A few hours later, Jenny came over with her wet suit on and told me to take a break. She would cover for me while I ate and took a nap.

Chapter 4

The next morning, I woke at sunrise. I got dressed in a wet suit and headed toward the deck pool. The young dolphin squirmed around in Jenny's arms.

"Thank goodness you are here!" Jenny exclaimed.

"I'm guessing you had a rough night," I said.

"This dolphin is strong and restless, especially for an injured dolphin," she replied, glancing at the dolphin, then looking back at me. "I'm surprised you survived a day with her."

I glanced down at the young bottlenose dolphin and said, "She was a sweetie for me."

I slipped into the water, and the dolphin started to click and whistle happily. She fought her way out of Jenny's arms and swam happily over to me. She rubbed up against me like a cat would with its owner. Jenny climbed out of the water and grabbed a towel. I told her to go get some rest, that I would handle the dolphin. I looked at the dolphin and gently stroked her nose.

"We have to give you some x-rays today to check for infections," I said to the dolphin.

The young dolphin did not like this idea much, or maybe she just felt me tense up. She squealed a high-pitched sound that stayed in the air. Roxy, Rose, and Jenny came rushing over to see what happened.

"Hi, guys!" I said.

"What was that?" they said.

"That was this little dolphin getting worked up when I told her she was getting x-rays today. I am not sure if it is the word, or if she can just feel my nerves."

Once again, the dolphin let out a squeal high enough to blow out an ear-drum. All three girls plugged their ears.

"Well, she obviously doesn't like something," Rosy said with a smile, almost giggling.

Jenny walked over to the cooler and grabbed a bucket. She filled the cooler with fish and brought it over to me. I took a fish out of the bucket and handed it to the dolphin, who gobbled it up. I could tell that made her happy. The young dolphin started to whistle that same song I sang to her yesterday.

"Wait. Is that 'Hush Little Baby' she's whistling?" Jenny said.

"Yep!" I answered happily.

"How does she know that song?" Rosy asked.

I replied proudly, "I sang it to her yesterday."

Jenny stared at me, her eyes wide. "You certainly have a special bond with that dolphin."

I smiled, thinking to myself how right she was.

We took the dolphin down to the surgical room in the sling to get an x-ray, being careful not to say the word "x-ray." After doing a few scans, we found why she was injured so severely. You could tell she had been entangled in fishing line on her upper peduncle (part of her tail), around her pectoral flipper (side flipper), and to her lower peduncle. There was no more fishing line, just deep cuts showing where the fishing line had been. We saw the cuts but needed an x-ray to make sure there was nothing more. It meant a fisherman or diver had tried to rescue her and gotten all the fishing line off. Or maybe she had managed to loosen the fishing line on her own, and it slowly fell off. Either way, it was not a good scenario, and all four of us knew that. The cuts could get infected and cause serious harm. I studied the x-rays with the captain who is a marine biologist and found most of the wounds to be fine except for one. The gash on the upper peduncle was seriously infected.

We treated her with an antibiotic medicine and brought her back to the pool. Usually dolphins heal quickly, but when an infection sets in like this, it can be deadly. I slipped back into the water to keep her company. The young dolphin squealed in pain every time I touched her. I felt bad every time I heard her little whistle. I heard thunder in the distance and knew I had to hurry up.

Jenny came jogging to the poolside. When she came close to the pool's edge, she came to a halt.

"Lily, there is a really bad storm just a few miles away," Jenny said, looking at me with a panicked expression. I saw that look every time she became stressed out.

I looked out at the angry, dark sea swirling and crashing. I saw a bolt of lightning come down somewhere in the distance. I knew I was going to have to get out of the deck pool, but I didn't want to leave the dolphin. I counted the short seconds until I replied. *One, two, three, four, five.*

"I can't leave her," I said, looking into Jenny's eyes. I saw them change from panic to hurt, almost like those words cut into her.

"Lily, she'll be fine. It's not worth risking your life for a dolphin."

Those words cut into me. The truth hurt. There was a possibility that the dolphin wouldn't make it, but I couldn't face that. I couldn't let this dolphin die, but I also knew my staying in the water would not save her; it was just a comfort measure. In the two days I had known her, she had become a part of me—a part of me I couldn't let go. She was more than just an injured dolphin to me; she was my friend.

I stared at Jenny.

She sighed and looked worried. "Will you at least get out of the water?" she replied.

"Fine." I gave in.

I started to climb out of the water, but the dolphin grabbed my foot in her beak and pulled me back in. Jenny watched and giggled as this happened repeatedly.

I glared at her and said, "Instead of standing there doing nothing, you should try to help me out!"

She looked at me and stifled a laugh but got a fish and threw it into the water. This distracted the dolphin long enough for me to get out of the pool. Jenny handed me a bag. I looked inside. There were a towel, a beach ball, a change of clothes, some food, my phone, and, lastly, my beloved diary. Jenny said, "I knew I could get you out, but I also knew you wouldn't leave. So I went to your room and got you some stuff."

"Thank you so much," I said, looking at her.

"I thought you might have needed that stuff."

I smiled, taking out the towel. Thunder roared, and we both stood under umbrellas on the side of the pool deck.

"Thanks," I said. "You're the best."

Chapter 5

I stood at the edge of the pool deck, watching the dolphin swim around for a couple more minutes. I decided it was best for me to take cover under the boat canopy by the door leading inside. I could still see the dolphin, but I knew how lightning was in Florida. The rain poured down, and large waves rocked the boat. The thunder rumbled, and the dolphin squeaked. I took my diary out of the bag Jenny gave me. After opening it to the next blank page, I wrote,

Dear Diary,

It is the evening of June 4. Sorry for the lack of updates. I have been really busy with this dolphin. We rescued her yesterday, and she is already my best friend. I'm on the dock right now, watching her. I haven't named her yet, but I think she really needs a name, so that's why I'm writing in you. So here are some name suggestions I have come up with.

Fluke, Song, Splash, Nellie, Whistle, Bubbles, Melody, Kelp, or Bella. I think I really like the name Melody. I think that will be her name.

All of a sudden, a splash of water hit my journal. It was soaked and probably ruined. I choked back a few sobs. "Melody! How could you? This journal has my entire life in it, and you just go and splash it!" Melody went under the water, came back up, and squirted me. The cool water hit my nice, dry clothes, and I was pissed. "Quit it! Why can't you just behave! All I've done is try to save your life, and this is what I get!" I got up, collected my things, and ran to my cabin. Tears streamed down my face. I curled up on my bed and cried. I felt Jenny sit next to me, and she put her hand on my back. It made me feel better that she cared, but my journal was ruined, and I was heartbroken.

The next morning, I walked out onto the dock. The storm was over, and the ocean was calm. Across the deck, I could see Melody swimming around in circles in the pool. I knew I should probably apologize, because she hadn't meant to ruin my journal; all she wanted was attention. I walked over to the pool, and Melody happily spy-hopped (she peeked her head out of the water and looked around) like nothing happened yesterday.

I smiled and rubbed the top of her head and said, "I'm so sorry. I never meant anything I said. I was just really upset about my journal."

Melody looked at me, her small black eyes glowing with happiness. I slid into the water and treated her cuts. I was so glad I had my best friend back, but I still had to figure out a way to make it up to her. There had to be some way. I got it: extra fish. Melody—well, any dolphin—loved fish more than anything. So she got an extra fish! She was happy, I thought, but I couldn't be sure, especially as she would probably be happiest when she felt better and could swim free. I swam with her just like all the other times, but now she was starting to feel better and wanted to play. She kind of reminded me of a little kid that was not feeling well, but once the medicine kicked in, she got her energy back.

I sang her a few more songs, which she squeaked and whistled back to me. This is why I thought Melody was a great name. She had this crazy ability to hear sounds and almost mimic them. I had never heard of any dolphin doing this before, but maybe Melody was special. I was scared to bring this to the captain's attention, because he would probably think I was crazy. I figured for now it could kind of be our little secret. I had no clue how I'd gotten so mad at this dolphin yesterday, but I *was* upset about my journal.

After a while, Roxy came out of the cabin to tell me to go eat lunch. I got out of the pool and grabbed a towel. After finishing a sandwich inside, I came back out to the most shocking sight I'd ever seen. Rose was hovering over her sister, Roxy, who was bleeding. Roxy's arm was dripping blood, and her shoulder was gashed open. Rose and Jenny hoisted Roxy up off the ground and moved her to a chair on the deck. There were a few mild cuts on her leg, but nothing was as bad as her shoulder. I had never seen so much blood come out of a human being until now. The worst part was I had never seen Roxy cry until now, either.

After standing there in shock, I finally rushed over to help out. I asked Jenny, "What can I do to help? What the heck happened?"

She looked at me and said in a panicked voice, "Go ask Captain Frank where the doctor is."

I ran down to the captain's cabin and banged on the door. " Captain Frank, Captain Frank, come here! It's an emergency, Frank!"

Frank opened the door, and I fell flat on my face into his cabin. I hastily got up.

"Are you OK? Are the other girls OK? What's going on?" he said, looking around frantically.

"I'm OK. Jenny and Rose are OK. Roxy is not OK," I replied.

"What happened? Is she dead? Is she sick? Is she injured? Do we need a doctor?"

I honestly had no idea how he became our ship's captain. He got so stressed out.

"We do need the ship's doctor, and we need you to calm down!"

He sighed. "OK, I will do both." He turned around and yelled, "Emily, the girls need you. Bring your doctor stuff."

Emily grabbed a kit she'd prepared and rushed out of the cabin. I followed her as she ran upstairs to the deck. She quickly got to where Roxy, Rose, and Jenny were.

"What on earth happened to her?" Emily said, looking at Roxy.

"We don't know, Doctor. We were on the other side of the dock and heard her scream," Jenny said.

I watched as Melody swam around the pool, watching us. She whistled softly, but I could make out "Hush, little baby, don't you cry," as if she knew what was going on. She watched as Emily stitched up Roxy's arm and gently wrapped it. Roxy calmed down as the doctor began to treat the smaller cuts on her leg.

"What happened?" I asked as Roxy sat in the chair, watching diligently as Emily put medicine on her cuts.

"That dolphin!"

I looked at her, confused. "Melody? She wouldn't hurt a fly!" I said, looking at Melody with a "no you didn't" look on my face.

"Right after you left, she freaked out. I tried to calm her down, but she started to slap her tail on the water. I didn't want her to hurt her tail worse, so I grabbed on to her tail. She whirled around and bit me. Her bite was strong, and she didn't let loose. She started tearing at me."

I stared, shocked. Really?

"Melody would never do that on purpose. She just gets riled up," Jenny said.

Emily lifted Roxy out of the chair and carried her down to the surgical cabin. I sat on the deck with my feet dangling in Melody's pool. Jenny and Rose sat next to me on their knees, not daring to put a toe in the water. I whistled, and Melody swam over.

"What did you do?"

Melody put her head underwater and started shaking it frantically from side to side. Oh, I loved this dolphin.

"OK, OK."

She came back up, whistling. Her squeaks were sad and scared.

"Melody, it's OK. It's not your fault," I said.

Jenny and Rose looked at me as if I were crazy.

"Really? That dolphin almost killed my sister, and you're all sweet and kind to her? I mean, maybe a little respect would be nice." Rose blew up at me.

"Yeah, OK, blame Melody. Your sister was as wrong as Melody," I retorted.

"Oh, yeah? I don't see the dolphin gushing blood, do I? I see a little dolphin who is as guilty as can be!" she said, pure anger in her voice.

Her words were sharp. If it hadn't been about Melody, I would have backed down.

"Since when is it OK to grab a dolphin's tail fluke when it's already angry?" I said.

Rose said, "When you're in pure panic, it's a natural response."

I hated her right now. "Rose, leave me alone. OK?"

Rose got up and stomped away.

"Jenny?" I said.

"I'm still here," she said.

I leaned on her shoulder and started to cry softly.

Chapter 6

The next morning, I woke up in my cabin bed, all tucked in and snuggled up. I hoped the last two days had been a dream. I ran to the drawer I left my diary in and opened it. I sighed when I realized the diary was still ruined. I grabbed it and opened it to my very first entry, from when I was just eight years old.

Dear Diary,

Well, I know what I want to be when I grow up. A marine biologist. You know, those people who go out and study dolphins?

That's going to be me. I hope my best friend is a dolphin. I've read lots of stories about girls who befriend dolphins and the dolphins help them. If only I could speak dolphin! Could you imagine that? Today I watched the dolphins at the dolphin rehab. I felt bad for some of the dolphins. Their stories were sad. I hope they are returned to the ocean soon and can continue living the lives they had before getting caught in fishing nets. Anyway, this is my first entry because I want to see if I can fulfill this dream when I get older.
—Lily

I smiled to myself as I looked at my old hand-writing, all smudged now. I still planned on fulfilling that dream, though, more now than I ever expected I would. I ripped out the pages of my first entry and the pages of my last entry. After stapling them together, I put them in a small box and shut it. Then I got out of my PJs and dressed quickly. I grabbed what was left of my diary and ran onto the deck.

Once I reached the railing, I looked down into the deep blue waves. Gripping my diary tightly, I decided I could be OK without it. I walked into the doorway and threw my diary in the trash. I turned away and walked down the hall. I knocked on the cabin door that Roxy was in to check on how she was doing. I opened the door slowly and walked in. Rose was crying, Jenny was on the phone, and Emily was wrapping Roxy's arm. Jenny finally hung up and looked at me, knowing I wanted an explanation.

"Roxy's shoulder cuts are bad, and she has begun to go into shock. She has also begun to run a fever. We don't want to wait, so I just called for a helicopter to come pick her up and bring her to the hospital," she said.

Emily looked up. "What time is the helicopter supposed to get here?" she asked.

"Eleven a.m. at the latest. That gives us two hours," Jenny replied.

I looked at Roxy, who looked scared. "Will I be OK?" she said.

I looked at her and said, "I don't know, but we sure hope so."

She sighed and said, "Don't blame any of this on Melody. It wasn't her fault."

Rose looked at me and whispered, "I'm sorry."

I whispered back, "It's OK, and I'm sorry too."

Rose stood up. "I'll go pack Roxy up." Then she walked out of the room and closed the door behind her.

I got up and patted Roxy. "If anyone can handle this, it is you. Stay strong," I said, a little choked up.

"Thanks." Then Roxy looked at Emily. "Can you get me what I made last night?"

Emily rolled back in her chair and grabbed a paper.

"I made this for you. Happy early birthday," Roxy said.

I took the paper. A dolphin was drawn on the front. Smiling, Roxy watched me look at her drawing.

"You did this with one hand?"

Roxy smiled and said, "Yes. My drawing arm isn't hurt."

I said, "Thanks," and cried. Jenny was smiling. She knew Roxy and I were very close. "You going to be OK?"

Before I could answer, the door opened, and Rose dropped a suitcase on the floor. "Done," she said.

"We only have an hour. We should probably start saying good-bye," I said.

Jenny went up to Roxy and said good-bye and wished her luck. Then it was my turn. I didn't know what to say. It was hard for me to come up with words. "Roxy, you will be fine. I love you so much, and don't be nervous."

Then I let Rose say good-bye. Jenny and I decided to leave them alone and wait for the helicopter. All of a sudden, I heard the helicopter. They slowly moved the helicopter close to the boat. Emily and Captain Frank walked Roxy out on the deck. They lowered a long basket from the helicopter for Roxy to lie down in. One of the coast guard medics was also lowered to the boat deck. After she was loaded and strapped in, they slowly began to pull her up. It was so loud and windy. I had never experienced a helicopter this close. Water was splashing everywhere; it was kinda scary.

The other man from the coast guard was then pulled up in his harness. He was pulled in, and they began to fly away.

We all stared, and I said, "I hope she gets better quick."

I went in the door and back downstairs. When I got to my cabin, I put Roxy's drawing in my drawer. I slipped on my wet suit and walked back out on the deck. Jenny was sitting on a beach chair next to Melody's pool.

"What are you doing?" I asked.

I saw her fidget a bit. Then she replied, "Just trying to clear my mind."

I climbed down the ladder into Melody's pool. Melody swam up happily and splashed me a few times. Then she swam behind me and pushed her rostrum against my back. I turned around, and she went underwater to start blowing bubbles. When she came up, she let out a loud squeal and started to spyhop. All of a sudden, I saw a large male dolphin breach near the boat.

"Whoa!" Jenny was already leaning over the edge.

I climbed out of the pool and stood next to her. "Hurry up and grab the camera. If you open the door, it is on the back side, hanging on the hook." The dolphin jumped and rode the bow waves for a while before disappearing.

I was able to take some good pictures. I went back downstairs to view the photos I got, but Jenny stayed up on deck. What was with her? Why didn't she care about the photos? I flipped through my camera and found two really good ones that I just loved. I loaded them onto my computer and then printed them out. I hung them on my wall next to some photos of Melody and other dolphins.

Then I fell asleep until morning...until my birthday! I was finally twelve!

"Lily, get up!" Jenny was tugging at my arm.

"OK." I got out of bed, and Jenny pulled me onto the deck. There was a huge banner that said **HAPPY BIRTHDAY LILY** in big, bold capital letters!

"You did this all for me?" I said.

"Yep. Follow me. Rose and I got you presents, too!"

I followed her to Melody's tank. I walked over, and Melody used her nose to push a box toward me.

I opened the present, and it was a new diary. I looked at her in disbelief. "How?"

She said, "I got it for you before we even left. I had no idea your diary would be damaged, but I figured since you had it so long, it must be getting full. Please keep this one in your room."

Wow. I held the book in my hand. A small dolphin was engraved on the front, and it said, "Lily's Diary." I laughed and opened to the first page. It read, "Lots of Love, Jenny + Rose + Melody."

"Thank you, guys, so much."

Jenny then placed a small gold box in my hand. A dolphin was painted on the front. I opened it up, and there was a metal dolphin tail on a chain. Not just any dolphin tail—to me it looked just like Melody's tail. When we got home, I was going to get it engraved with "Melody: the song of the ocean."

"Thank you so much! It's beautiful, Jenny!"

I put the necklace around my neck; it fit perfectly. Then Rose tapped me on the shoulder and handed me a larger box. Inside was a small ceramic dolphin.

"Wow! Thank you, Rose!"

I sat on the edge of Melody's pool, talking to Jenny and Rose, for the rest of the day. I really wished Roxy was there. Before I went to bed, I drew a quick picture of Melody in my diary. Her cuts were healing, and I knew that eventually it would be good-bye. I shook my head. We couldn't worry about that yet. Then I put my diary on my desk, climbed into bed, and fell asleep.

Chapter 7

I opened my eyes. The cabin was dark, and I could hear Jenny snoring. I looked at the clock. 4:05 a.m.

"Well, that is great, just great," I muttered under my breath.

I felt wide awake, though, and had no plans of going back to bed. I rolled over and took off my covers. I quickly changed into my wet suit and slipped on the necklace Jenny got me. I had decided I would wear it every day. I opened the door slowly, hoping it wouldn't creak, and slipped out of the room. I climbed the stairs as quietly as I could and went onto the deck. As soon as Melody saw me, she whistled.

"Shhhhh," I said. "You might wake the others!"

She quieted down. When I got closer, I noticed that she looked almost sad, not swimming with strength. I knew something was wrong, but couldn't see anything. I needed the other girls now! I ran down the stairs and flung open the door to the cabin Jenny and I shared.

"Jenny! Wake up, wake up!" I yelled.

"OK, I'm up. What time is it?" she muttered, still half-asleep.

"Five a.m., but something is wrong with Melody!" I said.

As soon as I said that, Jenny was out of bed. We ran to wake Rose. We all ran up the cabin stairs and back outside.

"Oh my gosh" was all Jenny said when she saw Melody.

"Do you think it has something to do with yesterday?" I said.

Jenny shook her head in thought. "I don't know, but I think we should wake Captain Frank," she said finally.

I didn't get in the water. I didn't want to do any further harm if something was wrong. We needed to wait for the captain; he was the marine biologist, so he would know what to do.

When Captain Frank arrived, he said, "She does not look so good." Captain Frank started looking her over. The infected upper peduncle was looking much better and beginning to heal. "Girls, we need to draw some blood." The captain then left to get some supplies from the surgical cabin. He returned about fifteen minutes later. The captain got in the water while I stood by the side of Melody. The captain took some blood so he could begin running tests. Melody seemed really quiet. I was hoping nothing bad was happening to her. She really was the best thing that had ever happened to me.

I sat on the edge of the pool and watched her swim around slowly. She seemed calm today. I watched as she came up to the surface and took a breath. Her cuts were still visible but looked much better. I looked around at the ocean, where I saw a few fish jumping in the rough water. It looked as though a storm was heading in. It was getting windier and windier. When I looked up, the sky that used to be blue was now a dark gray. The waves were now very high. I sat under the overhang by the door and tried to stay calm. All of a sudden, I heard footsteps running up the stairs. Jenny came onto the deck and yelled, "LILY... REAL BIG STORM...COME NOW."

I got up and looked at Melody. She flipped her tail as if she were waving good-bye, so I reluctantly ran across the deck to where Jenny was standing. Then we slowly descended. Jenny and I went into our cabin. After a small game of checkers (I won), we went into the underwater viewing center. We watched small fish swim by, then a hammerhead shark and large loggerhead turtle. The best part was that we got it on video. The video didn't do it justice. Then, all of a sudden, the underwater room shook, and there was a large thump. Jenny and I whirled around to see a large female bull shark, who didn't seem too happy.

"Jenny—" I started to say. Then there was another thud. "I think she's mad," I finished.

I looked at Jenny. She had her video camera out and was recording the bull shark. "JENNY!" I yelled.

"THIS IS AWESOME," she replied.

I shook my head and watched as the bull shark attacked two more times before swimming away. I looked at Jenny, who had a huge smile on her face. Then we both ran to our cabin to check out the footage. We loaded it onto the computer and watched it five times. It was so cool. I looked down at the dolphin-tail necklace around my neck and smiled to myself. Jenny went on the top bunk to read. It was a good way to pass the time.

Suddenly there was a knock on the door. It was the captain. "Girls, can you come here for a minute?" We opened the door went down the hall and got Rose. The captain looked at all of us and said, "Let's go sit at the table in the dining hall." We agreed. He said, "These are the results of blood work," and laid out the papers. We didn't understand them, but the captain went through them with us, and the bottom line was all tests had come back fine. He thought she was just really stressed from what had happened with Roxy. We all were thrilled with the news. Jenny and I said we were going back to our room for a bit, hoping the rain would pass.

When we got back to the room, I decided now was a good time to talk to Jenny about some stuff.

"Jenny," I said.

"Yes," she replied.

"I'm sorry," I said and sat down.

She looked at me funny and said, "For what?"

I sighed and said, "For not spending as much time with you. Ever since Melody came, I have kind of isolated myself with her. I didn't mean to, but I did. And now Melody is getting better and will be released soon, and I have kind of pushed you away."

Jenny looked at me and smiled. "Lily, trust me, I want you to spend as much time as you want with Melody. I really do. Melody isn't going to be with you forever, and eventually you will have to say good-bye, but you need to treasure every moment you have with her until then. Don't worry about me. I'll always be here. Trust me."

She climbed down and hugged me. I smiled. As we both went to bed, I sat and listened to the rain and let that lull me into sleep.

The next morning, I woke up and slipped on my wet suit and my dolphin-tail necklace.

Then I ran up the stairs to find Melody waiting for me. She already seemed to be getting back to her normal self. I climbed into the pool and gave Melody a big hug. She whistled and then wiggled out of my arms. She started to swim in circles, round and round and round, faster and faster and faster. All of a sudden, she went zooming out of the water, jumped about five feet in the air, and then came crashing down, soaking me. The water from the splash sloshed over the sides of the pool and poured off the side of the boat. Seconds later she was underwater, playing with my feet. I called Jenny, who quickly came with a beach ball for us to play with. Melody seemed happy and energetic, so I decided to play a game of catch with her. After a while, Melody was bored of catch, so we just swam around together.

Chapter 8

Dear Diary,

I love Melody. She's one of a kind. Jenny told me to take a break and a nap today, but I'm bored and don't know what to do because lately all I've done is hang out with Melody. Maybe I'll go talk to Captain Frank, if he's not too busy with his captain duties.

I closed my diary and ran toward the captain's room. I knocked three times.

"Come in," I heard Frank yell. He was sitting at his table drinking soda.

"Hey!" I said.

He looked at me and asked, "How's Melody?"

I smiled. "Well, she's doing so much better."

Frank nodded. "That is great. I will need to go down soon and check on her myself."

I smiled and nodded excitedly. "Of course, but maybe in an hour. Right now, can we just hang out? Jenny's taking care of Melody."

Frank smiled and said, "Sure," and then he got up and poured me a glass of water, knowing how much I hated soda. We sat down and chatted for a while about our itinerary. We couldn't go too far, because we had Melody.

Then Jenny came in and said that I could go back to Melody now. She seemed tired, but I decided not to ask questions.

Melody was so happy to see me. She started splashing and whistling with some dancing.

"Now I know why you call her Melody," Frank said, laughing as he listened to her whistle a lullaby. Frank petted her and played with her from the deck. Melody was overjoyed to have me back in the pool with her. After a lot of swimming around in the dolphin pool, I got out and dried off on the beach chairs and watched as Melody pushed around the beach ball.

After we spent a few minutes chatting, the sun started to go down, and Frank went down to his cabin. I watched as he went, and then I turned to Melody, threw her a fish, and waved good-bye. As I went across the deck, I watched as the sky went from red and orange to pink. I went downstairs to go to bed. I was exhausted and wanted to get up early the next morning. I took off my necklace and put on my PJs. Jenny asked why I was going to bed so early, and I told her I was tired. She shrugged but didn't ask questions. I lay in bed until I fell asleep.

The next morning, I got up at five, just like I'd wanted to. I grabbed a mop and marched upstairs to the upper deck. I felt like the place needed a cleaning, so why not clean it? After two hours of mopping, I got into Melody's pool and scrubbed it down with a sponge. Melody was annoyed by not getting attention. She kept swimming around me, nudging me, poking me, and grabbing my sponge.

"Melody!" I said when she grabbed my sponge.

She was already on the other side of the pool with it. I swam over and grabbed the sponge from her, and then went back to scrubbing. After she had stolen the sponge from me three times, I gave up. I was done with most of the cleaning by the time the others woke up. I watched as Jenny and Rose walked onto the sparkling-clean deck.

"Whoa, this is clean!" Jenny exclaimed.

Then Rose said, "You did all this?"

I smiled proudly and said, "Yeah, I got up early to surprise you guys."

Jenny and Rose looked amazed.

"Let's go show Frank and Em," Rose said. Rose was very close to Emily and called her Em. Everyone else on the boat called her Dr. Emily.

"Are you sure they're up?" I replied.

"Well, it's nine. They should be," Jenny said.

Jenny, Rose, and I walked down the cabin stairs and toward the captain's room. If one of them was up, it would be Frank, so we went to his room first.

We knocked, and Frank yelled, "Who is it?"

"Um, Lily, Jenny, and Rose," I yelled through the door.

"All three of you?" he yelled back.

"Yes. Will you just open the door?" Jenny rolled her eyes.

Frank opened the door. "Good morning," he said.

"Good morning," we girls said in sync.

"Follow us," Jenny said.

"OK," Frank said, stepping out of his cabin.

We led him upstairs to the deck I'd just cleaned.

"Ta-da," I said.

Frank stared. "Wow" was all he said.

That morning I actually ate breakfast with everyone. When Emily got to breakfast, Frank said, "Did you see what Lily did?"

Emily looked at us weirdly and said, "No."

I smiled. "It's on the upper deck. I'll show you when we're done eating."

Emily nodded.

"What made you come down and eat with us today?" Frank asked.

I replied, "I got up early and felt like hanging out a bit before going to Melody."

Frank nodded.

"How is Melody?" Rose asked.

"She's doing really well! We might be able to release her by next week. Then we can finish up the rest of the trip. Her cuts are healing quickly, and she doesn't have the infection anymore," I answered.

Jenny looked at me, knowing how hard it was going to be for me to say good-bye. She patted me on my shoulder. When we were done eating, I showed Emily the deck.

"Nice! It's as good as new."

When Emily left, I slipped into the pool to play with Melody. Melody swam up and spit water at me. I ducked under and came up, splashing her, which started an all-out splash battle. Melody squealed and jumped and swam and then splashed some more. When she finally settled down a bit, I decided to feed her. This time, though, instead of giving her a dead fish, I reached into a bucket and pulled out a large fish that was still alive and healthy.

"If you want it, you'll have to catch it, like when you were in the big ocean," I said and then placed the fish in the water.

Melody bolted after the fish and quickly caught it!

"Good girl, Melody! All right. Now, get these three," I said as I put three more live fish in the water.

She gobbled all three up after a ten-second chase.

"Nice," I said.

Then I got a cardboard figure of a fisherman and put it next to the dolphin pool. Melody quickly swam to the other side of the pool.

"Well, I guess you know to stay away from humans you don't know," I said, laughing.

Then I went back into the pool to play with her. She happily swam around me. At noon, I went down and ate lunch with everyone again. I wanted to tell them about the training I did with Melody to prepare her for release.

"Hey, guys!" I said when I got down to the cabin.

"Hi, Lily."

I sat down and ate my sandwich.

"Guys, I have good news! Melody still remembers how to hunt and to stay away from humans she doesn't know," I said excitedly.

"That's great, Lily! When will she be ready to be released?"

I thought for a minute. "Probably by Sunday, but I think we should release her on Monday." I paused and then added, "That way I have an extra day to say good-bye."

Frank nodded. "I think it may be better if we release her on Sunday, because then we can start on our way up to Virginia to see the whales on Monday." Frank surprised us with this. We thought all we would study was dolphins, but now we would see some whales too. This was the best camp ever!

I sighed. It was worth a try, I thought.

"Are you sure we can't wait one more day? You know how much Lily is going to miss Melody," Jenny said.

I smiled.

Frank thought for a minute. "I don't think so. We want to make it there as soon as possible."

"OK," I said, disappointed. I finished my sandwich quickly and said good-bye to everyone. Then I rushed out of the room. I had only two more days with Melody, and I needed to make the most of them. I slipped into the water and gave Melody a kiss. I thought back to when I had first met her. That was almost one month ago. Now she was healed and was going back to the ocean, her home. I was going to miss her a lot, but I knew she had to go. Melody was my best friend. Best friends love each other no matter how many miles apart.

"Two days," I said to myself.

Melody must have sensed my sad mood, because she started to whistle softly and swim slowly around the tank.

Chapter 9

The next morning, I woke up and frowned. Tomorrow Melody was going home. I knew I should be happy, that my hard work had paid off, but I couldn't help but think that I would never see her again.

"Jenny, are you up?" I whispered.

"Yeah," she said.

"I have to say good-bye to Melody tomorrow, and it's going to be hard."

Jenny sighed. "It's not good-bye. It's 'see you later.'"

I thought for a minute. "It's good-bye," I said.

"You can't be sure," Jenny replied.

I walked to the pool sadly. But when I saw Melody, she put a smile on my face. She was spy-hopping, but then I noticed something else. There were other dolphins…who were jumping. They knew. They knew she was coming home. It was her pod. Melody chattered back and forth with one of the dolphins.

"JENNY!" I yelled.

Jenny came running up the stairs.

"Whoa! Is this a dolphin party?" Jenny exclaimed when she saw the five dolphins and Melody.

"It's time," I whispered.

"Time for what?" Jenny asked.

"Time to release Melody," I replied.

Jenny called Rose, and I called Frank. They came up. I got the sling. As I slipped into the water, a tear dripped down my face. I kissed Melody on her soft forehead and whispered, "Be safe." I slipped the sling under her, and Rose helped me lift her out of the water. Then we both lowered her into the ocean. She hesitated for a second but then swam out of the sling to her pod. I watched as she played with her family. She swam happily and leaped. Eventually, though, they wanted to leave. Melody swam up to the edge of the boat where I was standing and whistled. I reached down and patted her small forehead. "Good-bye, Melody," I said and watched as she and her dolphin friends swam away, without me, leaving me behind. Soon, they were out of sight.

Jenny hugged me and said, "She's home now."

Chapter 10

Lunchtime was quieter than normal. I had little to say. Frank told us how he was going to start to travel toward Virginia by five o'clock. We told him OK; then we headed down to the cabins. I had Melody's tail-fluke necklace around my neck. Jenny noticed and said, "It will remind you of her. It's something that will never let you forget her. You will always remember her when it's around your neck."

I nodded and replied, "I'm always going to remember her. I will never forget her." Then I continued. "Do you think she will remember me?"

Jenny smiled. "She will never forget."

I laughed and then opened up my diary.

Melody=Happiness
Melody=Love
Melody=Forever

I'd miss her, but now she was in the ocean, in her home.

"I think it's funny you released her a day early," Jenny said.

"Why?" I said, confused.

"Well, you wanted to release her on Monday, but Frank said Sunday, but then you released her Saturday," she said, laughing.

"I couldn't wait another day. Her family was waiting for her," I said, smiling.

"Yeah, they were," Jenny said and then continued. "I got her release on video, and I got video of her and her family!"

I rolled my eyes but smiled. "You get everything on video," I said.

"True," she said back. "Oh yeah, by the way, I've secretly been spying on you and taking videos of you and Melody," she said, smiling.

"Oh my gosh, you stalker!"

She burst out laughing. "Here, look." She showed me about an hour's worth of videos of me and Melody together.

"I thought you were kidding," I exclaimed.

"Nope," she said with an evil grin. "Also, on the days you took off, I got underwater footage of Melody."

Then she showed me about thirty minutes of Melody playing underwater.

"Aw, look at how cute she is," I said, smiling.

"Jenny, Lily, come up here now," we heard Rose yell.

Jenny and I looked at each other and ran. We saw it at the same time. We were heading straight toward rocks, and Frank was turning the wheel frantically, trying to turn the boat. I said to Frank, "Try to be calm. You will have better control." He turned the wheel, and we eventually moved just enough, narrowly missing the rocks. Once the rocks were past us, he straightened the boat back out.

"Um, almost a really bad situation," Frank muttered, embarrassed.

"Next time, calm down," I replied.

"Yeah. I'll have to work on that," he said.

Then I ran back to the girls to enjoy the water.

Jenny just smiled. The sun started to set, and we watched as it sank under the horizon till it was dark out; then we headed down to the cabins. Jenny and I went into ours and put on some music. We sang along and laughed hysterically every time we messed up the words. We played two games of checkers and ended up staying awake till three in the morning playing games. Eventually we decided to go to bed.

The next morning, we both missed breakfast, so we went down and ate together. We didn't go to the upper deck until eleven o'clock. The next three days went by like a blur. I spent a lot of this time with Jenny and Rose, getting our dolphin research done.

Now we were in Virginia, one of the best whale-watching places in the United States. We watched as the large whales surfaced. We even got to see them tail- and pec-slap (when whales slap their fins on the water)! It was incredible.

We stayed for another week studying whales, dolphins, and any other marine animals we got lucky enough to see, but all good things must come to an end. It was time for us to head back to the docks. It was the end of our trip. We had a few more days left at sea as Captain Frank turned us back toward Florida. Jenny and I headed down to the cabin to pack up. Jenny handed me a CD.

"What is this?" I asked.

"It's every video I took on the trip," she replied.

"Thank you so much!" I said. "I also have some really good news for you. Jenny, you know how I told you a while ago my parents wanted to sell our house and move to San Diego? Well, my mom just texted me, and my dad got a promotion, so we are staying. I'm so excited I couldn't wait to tell you. Now we will be able to do more studies together!"

"Is this a joke?" she said, looking at me, smiling.

"Nope!" I said.

She started jumping up and down. "We're going to have so much fun."

Rose was happy to hear the news, and she really liked the CD. Jenny gave her an extra one for Roxy, and then we gave both Emily and Frank one also.

The day had come, and the ship was pulling into the docks. I stood at the side of the boat with both girls by my side as we pulled in. I looked over at them and said, "I am so happy we all got into this camp together, made these memories, and built friendships that will last a lifetime." I turned and said, "Group hug," and began to cry. "I don't know if we will ever get to do something like this again, but we all must stay in touch, no matter what. Rose, please tell Roxy this also. We know she will have plenty to say, because she always does, so tell her we look forward to a call."

Jenny and I took our bags and hugged and thanked Emily and Captain Frank. We thanked them for picking us for this amazing journey, everything we had learned, and the time they spent teaching us. As we walked down the dock to leave the ship, I glanced over my shoulder for one more look at the *Dolphin Dancer*. Our families were all there to welcome us home and give us lots of hugs. My mom had so many questions for me on the drive home I almost needed another vacation. My little brother had a ton of things he wanted to tell me about. My dad—well, he just looked in the mirror and smiled. I could tell they were all happy to have me home.

The five-hour drive went really fast this time because we all had so much to say. Jenny and I had a movie night with both of our families! We put the CD into the DVD player and watched the whole trip. It was amazing, and her video skills were so good.

I still wear my Melody necklace every day and even got it engraved. I think about Melody a lot, too. I miss her so much. I wonder how she's doing, if she gets along with her pod mates, and if she's OK. Though I'm sure she is.

Dear Diary,

I haven't written since I got off the boat, but I just wanted to let you know everything is great since I have been home, and I have not forgotten about you. I've just been so busy. Roxy called the other day and said that her arm is doing much better, and she will be able to go on our next study expedition!

—Lily

About the Author

Gianna Perugini is a seventh-grade student from Trinity, Florida. She lives with her parents and younger brother.

Perugini wants to be a marine biologist and is already hard at work training for her chosen profession. She runs the @belugawhale_ fanpage account on Instagram. She loves studying cetaceans; rowing with her crew in Tampa, Florida; and spending time with her many fish and leopard gecko, Sammi.